Hop in.

Lock the doors.

Buckle up.

Let's go.

Look out!

SPLATTER !

SPLOSH !

MUDDY CAR.

Yippee!

CAR WASH

Sandra Steen
and
Susan Steen

illustrated by

G. Brian Karas

G. P. Putnam's Sons • New York

To our long-distant writer's group:
Merry Banks
Ellen Leroe
Connie Ryan
—S. S. & S. S.

For Rowan, Macklin and Galen
—G. B. K.

Text copyright © 2001 by Sandra Steen and Susan Steen
Illustrations copyright © 2001 by G. Brian Karas
All rights reserved. This book, or parts thereof, may not be reproduced in any form
without permission in writing from the publisher,
G. P. PUTNAM'S SONS
a division of Penguin Putnam Books for Young Readers,
345 Hudson Street, New York, NY 10014. G. P. Putnam's Sons, Reg. U.S. Pat. & Tm. Off.
Published simultaneously in Canada.
Printed in Hong Kong by South China Printing Co. (1988) Ltd.   Designed by Semadar Megged.
Text set in Kosmik. The artwork was prepared with gouache,
acrylics, pencil, and some odds and ends.
Library of Congress Cataloging-in-Publication Data
Steen, Sandra. Car wash / Sandra Steen and Susan Steen ; illustrated by G. Brian Karas. p. cm.
Summary: While sitting inside their car, two children enjoy the soapy sights and watery sounds of
the car wash. [1. Car washes—Fiction.] I. Steen, Susan. II. Karas, G. Brian, ill.
III. Title. PZ7.S8149 Car 2001 [E]—dc21 00-021402
ISBN 0-399-23369-5
1 3 5 7 9 10 8 6 4 2
First Impression

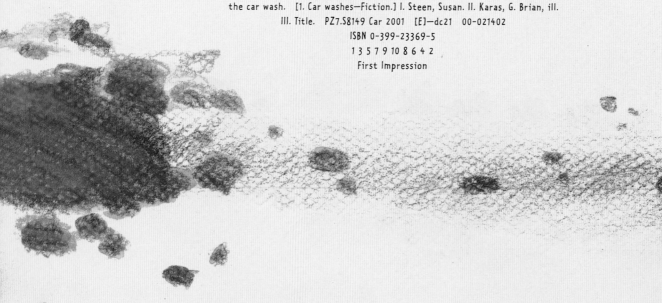

Car Wash →

Car wash.

Windows up.

Engine off.

On track.

Close hatch. Submarine.

Going down. Deep. Dark.

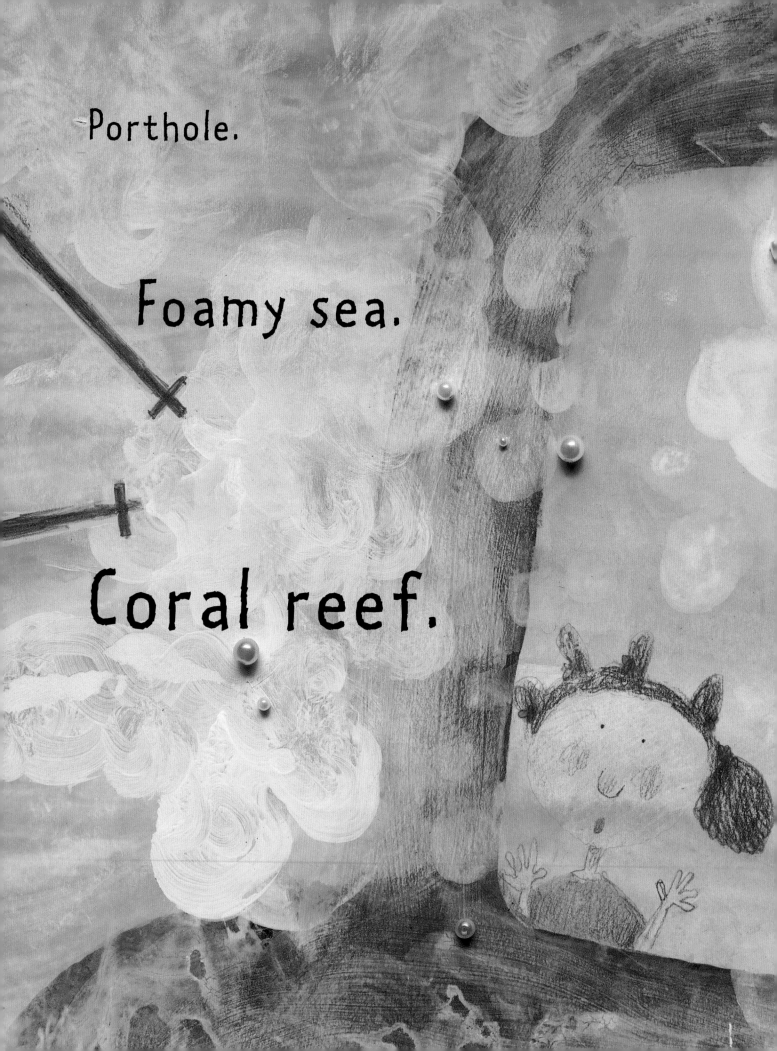

Porthole.

Foamy sea.

Coral reef.

What's that?

Giant arms.

Octopus.

WHOMP!

THOMP!

Big claws. Sea monster.

DON'T LOOK BACK

Close call.

Seaweed.

Creatures hide.

Sharks circle.
DON'T MOVE!

Tidal wave.

Hang on!

Psss!

Psss!

Safe
and sound.

Bubbles
dance.

Beads race.

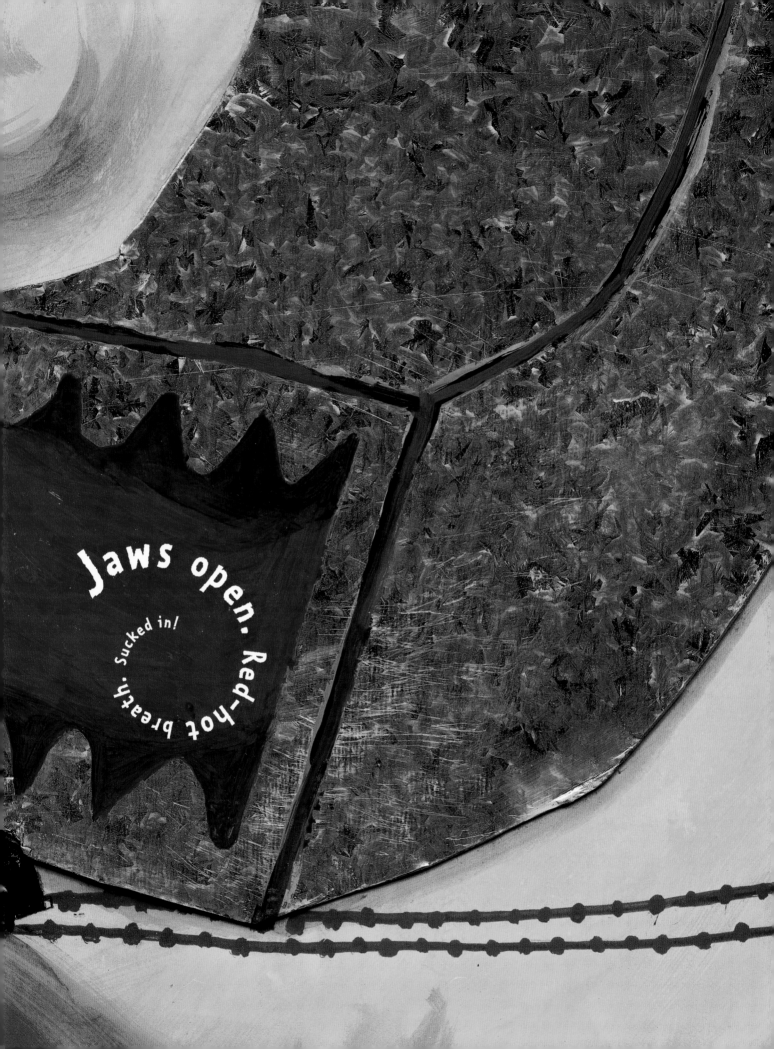

Jaws open. Red-hot breath. Sucked in!

HONK HONK!

Spit us OUT.

Going UP.

ALL CLEAR!

Drip,
drip.
Towel
dry.
Shiny
car.